THE GIRL IN THE BUSH

by Pantelis Giamouridis

Published by Pantelis Rafail Giamouridis

First Edition: April 2023

PROLOGUE

Dear Reader,

I am delighted to share this unique story with you and I would like to express my sincerest gratitude to each and every one of you.

In the pages that follow, you will immerse yourself in the world of Willowbrook, a town shrouded in secrets and mysteries. The story of Harper Bono, the retired detective turned reluctant hero, and his quest to unravel the enigma of "The Lost Children," is a tale that I have really enjoyed crafting and I hope it captures your imagination as much as it has mine!

This book was written with ESL learners in mind, and my goal was to create an engaging and accessible story that could be enjoyed by readers of varying language levels. I hope that, as you read, you will not only be drawn into the intriguing world of Willowbrook, but also find joy and inspiration in learning the English language.

I would like to express my gratitude to everyone who has supported this project, including my friends, family, and colleagues who have encouraged me throughout the writing process. Your enthusiasm and belief in my work have made this journey truly special.

Lastly, I invite you to stay tuned for future releases in this series, as there are many more captivating stories waiting to be told! Each installment will take you on a new and thrilling journey, exploring different genres such as classic retellings, mystery, adventure, and more. My aim is to offer something for everyone, while ensuring the stories are engaging, entertaining, and thought-provoking.

What sets this series apart is my commitment to cater to a wide range of language learners, aligning with the official CEFR levels of language learning.

This means that, regardless of your current language proficiency, you'll find stories that are just the right fit for your linguistic journey.

Once again, thank you for your support, and happy reading!

Warmest regards,

Pantelis Giamouridis

Chapter 1: A New Beginning

I'm Harper Bono, a retired detective with a bit of a past with drinking too much. For years, I roamed the streets of the city, solving cases and getting the bad guys. But as I got older and my energy began to fade, the noise and stress of the city became too much. So, I packed up my life and moved to a small, peaceful town called Willowbrook.

The day I arrived in the town, I could feel the peacefulness in the air. I walked around, looking at the houses and the people. They were friendly, waving and saying hello. I knew that this was the perfect place for me to start a new life.

As I moved into my new house, my neighbors came to help me. They brought food, smiles, and warm welcomes. I couldn't be more grateful. "Thank you," I said to them. "I'm happy to be part of this community."

One evening, I walked to the local store to buy some groceries. As I entered, I noticed a bulletin board near the entrance, filled with community news and announcements. While scanning the board, I spotted a flyer that caught my attention.

It was a picture of a young girl, smiling and wearing a bright red dress. The flyer read, *"Missing: Emily Johnson, 18 years old, last seen at the park on April 19th."* My heart sank as I read the words. Even though I was retired, my detective instincts kicked in, and I knew I had to help find her.

The next morning, I went to the town police station to learn more about the case. "Hello," I said to the officer at the desk. "I'm Harper Bono, a retired detective. I saw the flyer about Emily Johnson, and I'd like to help in any way I can."

The officer, a kind man named Peter, welcomed my help. "Thank you, Mr. Bono," he said. "We're a small team here, and we could use all the help we can get."

Peter gave me a brief overview of the case. Emily had been missing for three days, and her parents were frantic. They had searched the town and the surrounding woods, but there was no sign of her.

With the information in hand, I began my investigation. I started by talking to Emily's parents. They were kind people, and I could see the pain in their eyes. They told me about their daughter, how she loved to play video games and enjoyed reading mystery books. They couldn't imagine why anyone would want to hurt her.

Next, I visited the park where Emily was last seen. It was a lovely place, with tall trees, a playground, and a small pond. I carefully searched the area, looking for any clues that might lead me to Emily.

As I walked along the edge of the pond, I noticed something unusual. There, partially hidden by the tall grass, was a small red cloth. I picked it up and examined it. The color and texture were strikingly familiar. I suddenly remembered the photo of Emily I had seen at her parents' house, the one in which she was wearing a beautiful red dress. The memory of that photo was still vivid in my mind, as if it were etched into the very fabric of my thoughts.

The cloth I held in my hand was not just any piece of red fabric; it had a distinctive pattern of small white flowers that matched the dress in the photo. Additionally, it was obvious that the cloth had been torn off from something larger, rather than being a scrap that had been discarded. The edges were frayed, indicating that it had been ripped away with force.

As I continued to examine the piece of cloth, I recalled Emily's vibrant red hair and the way it contrasted with her dress in the photograph. The image had stayed with me for a while but I soon decided to return to the police station and show the cloth to Peter. "I found this near the pond in the park," I said. "It's from Emily's dress."

Peter's eyes widened. "This is a significant clue, Mr. Bono," he said. "We need to search that area again, more thoroughly."

Together, we organized a team of volunteers to search the park and the woods nearby. We spent the entire day combing the area, looking for any sign of Emily. But as the sun began to set, we still had no leads.

Feeling defeated, I returned to my house thinking about the case and the missing girl. I knew that I couldn't give up. My past experiences as a detective had taught me the importance of persistence and determination in solving cases. In my career, I had faced numerous dead ends and seemingly impossible situations, only to eventually uncover the truth through sheer determination and an unwillingness to give up. This case would be no different. But there were also times when, despite my best efforts, I couldn't save anyone.

As I sat in my chair, memories of past cases began to flood my mind. The faces of those I couldn't help haunted me, reminding me of the importance of never giving up, no matter how difficult the case may seem.
It was those unresolved cases and the people I couldn't save that drove me to push even harder in my search for the missing girl. I knew that I owed it to them, to Emily, and to myself to see this case through to the end.

I couldn't allow another unsolved case to weigh on my conscience, and I was determined to bring Emily home, no matter what obstacles stood in my way.

Chapter 2: Unraveling the Mystery

The next morning, I went to the town library to learn more about the town's history. I hoped that I might find some clues to help me solve Emily's disappearance. As I entered the library, a middle-aged woman named Alicia greeted me. She was the librarian and had lived in the town her entire life.

Alicia had a warm, welcoming smile that instantly put me at ease. Her eyes, framed by a pair of round glasses, were filled with kindness and intelligence. Her silver hair was pulled back into a neat bun, and she wore a simple yet elegant blouse and skirt. It was clear that she took great pride in her work at the library, as she moved gracefully among the shelves, her fingers lightly touching the spines of the books as if she knew each one intimately.

"Hello, dear," she said with a warm smile, her eyes lighting up with genuine interest. "What can I help you find today?"

I hesitated for a moment, not sure how much to reveal. Finally, I told her about Emily's case and my growing obsession with finding her. As I spoke, I watched Alicia's eyes fill with concern.

"I want to help you, Harper," she said softly, glancing around to make sure no one was listening. "Our town has a dark history of unsolved murders and disappearances. It's been going on for years, and I think I know who's responsible."

Alicia led me to a quiet corner of the library, away from the prying eyes and ears of other patrons. There, surrounded by dusty volumes of local history, she began to tell me about a shadowy organization called "The Lost Children." According to her research, this group was responsible for the unsolved crimes in the town. However, the police seemed to be either totally unaware of them or unwilling to pursue the matter further.

As I listened to Alicia's story, I felt a chill run down my spine. She described how the Lost Children operated in secret, their rituals and beliefs shrouded in mystery. It was said that they met in the depths of the nearby forest, performing sinister ceremonies under the cover of darkness. The more she spoke, the more I wondered - could this group be responsible for Emily's disappearance?

"I know it sounds crazy," Alicia admitted, her voice barely a whisper. "But I can't shake the feeling that they're involved somehow. If you're serious about finding Emily, you need to know what you're up against."

I thanked Alicia for her help, her words echoing in my mind as I left the library. The weight of the information she had shared weighed heavily on my shoulders, but it also fueled my determination.

I thanked Alicia for her help and left the library, determined to find out more about The Lost Children.

I spent the day searching for any information about the organization, but it seemed as if they didn't exist. No one in the town had heard of them, and there was no mention of them in the local newspapers. It was as if they were a ghost, a hidden secret that only Alicia knew about.

Feeling exhausted, I decided to pick up some groceries before returning home. As I approached my front door, I noticed something strange: the door was unlocked. My heart raced as I cautiously opened the door and stepped inside.

"Hello?" I called out, my voice shaking. There was no answer. I walked through the house, checking each room for any signs of an intruder. To my relief, everything seemed to be in order. Perhaps I had simply forgotten to lock the door earlier.

Despite the apparent safety, I couldn't shake the feeling that something was wrong. I decided to keep my discovery of the red cloth and my meeting with Alicia a secret, at least for the time being. I knew that if The Lost Children were responsible for Emily's disappearance, they might be watching me, too.

As I lay in bed that night, I couldn't help but think about the heresis and their connection to the town's dark history. I knew that I had to find out more if I wanted to solve the case and bring Emily home. But first, I had to make sure that I was safe from any potential threats.

I vowed to be more vigilant, to watch my surroundings and protect myself from harm. And with that promise, I closed my eyes and drifted off to sleep, ready to face the challenges that lay ahead.

Chapter 3: The Family and the Friend

The following day, I decided to pay another visit to Emily's family. I wanted to get a better understanding of the people in her life and the events leading up to her disappearance. As I approached their modest house, I could sense the heavy atmosphere surrounding it. The curtains were drawn, and the once well-tended garden now seemed neglected.

I knocked on the door, and Emily's father, a tall and stern man named Robert, answered. His eyes were red, and it was evident that he had been crying. "Mr. Bono, come in," he said, his voice trembling.

I entered the house and found Emily's mother, Mary, sitting in the living room. She looked fragile, her face pale, and her eyes filled with tears. She clutched a small, worn teddy bear, which I presumed belonged to Emily.

"Thank you for coming, Mr. Bono," Mary whispered. "We don't know what else to do."

I sat down beside her and assured her that I was doing everything in my power to find Emily. I asked them if they had any photos of Emily that I could take with me, hoping they might provide some clues.

Mary led me to Emily's room. It was a small but cozy space, filled with books, posters, and colorful drawings. She handed me a framed photo from the dresser. It was a picture of Emily, a beautiful red-haired girl with a bright smile that could light up a room. Her green eyes sparkled with happiness, and she wore the same red dress from the missing poster.

There were other people in the photo as well - a group of children around Emily's age, all smiling and laughing. I recognized a few of them as kids from the town, but one girl stood out to me. She was a blond girl named Monica, her arm wrapped around Emily's shoulders.

"Who is this girl?" I asked, pointing to Monica.

"Oh, that's Monica," Mary replied. "She and Emily are best friends. They did everything together. But since Emily disappeared, we haven't seen much of her."

I decided to pay a visit to Monica, hoping she might be able to provide some insight into Emily's life and her possible whereabouts. I thanked Emily's parents and left their house, the weight of their sorrow heavy on my heart.

With the help of some local residents, I located Monica's home - a small trailer parked at the edge of the town. As I approached, I noticed that the door was slightly ajar, and I could hear muffled voices coming from inside.

I knocked on the door, and a woman in her early thirties opened it. She introduced herself as Monica's mother and invited me in. The inside of the trailer was cramped, filled with mismatched furniture and an array of clutter.

In the corner, I spotted Monica, her blond hair pulled back into a ponytail. She was hunched over a sketchbook, her eyes red from crying. I introduced myself and explained that I was investigating Emily's disappearance.

Monica looked up at me, her eyes filled with fear and sadness. "I miss her so much," she whispered. "I just want her to come home."

I asked her if she had any idea where Emily might be or if she had noticed anything unusual leading up to her disappearance. Monica hesitated for a moment, her gaze drifting to the window.

"I don't know where she is," she finally said, her voice barely audible. "But the day before she disappeared, she seemed... worried. Like she was hiding something."

Before I could ask any more questions, I heard a commotion outside the trailer. I glanced out the window and saw Alicia, the librarian.Before I could ask any more questions, I heard a commotion outside the trailer. I glanced out the window and saw Alicia, the librarian. She was approaching with a sense of urgency, her chest heaving with each hurried breath. Her footsteps were uneven, almost stumbling, as if she was trying to run but her legs couldn't keep up with the frantic pace she wanted to maintain.

Monica didn’t seem particularly happy to see her.

Chapter 4: Unraveling Threads

I excused myself from the trailer and hurried outside to find Alicia. She looked out of breath, her face flushed from running. Monica followed me outside, her eyes narrowing as she saw Alicia.

"What are you doing here?" Monica snapped at her, her voice cold.

Alicia seemed unfazed by Monica's hostility. "I have some new information that might help find Emily," she said, her voice urgent. "I discovered a man named Trevor who might be connected to The Lost Children. He works at a bar outside town, and I think he might know something."

I considered Alicia's information, realizing it was a lead worth pursuing. Before I could respond, however, my phone rang. It was Peter from the police station.

"Mr. Bono, we've had another incident," he said, his voice tense. "Emily's house has been vandalized by a group of people. You need to come here right away."

I quickly thanked Alicia for her help and told her I would look into Trevor. Then, I rushed to Emily's house, my heart pounding in my chest.

As I approached the house, I saw a crowd of people gathered outside, their faces filled with shock and fear. I pushed my way through the crowd and stopped dead in my tracks when I saw the front door. It was spray-painted with the chilling words, "We found our way."

The atmosphere was thick with tension as the police tried to calm the onlookers and gather information. I spotted Peter and approached him. "Do you have any idea who did this?" I asked.

Peter shook his head, his face grim. "Not yet, but we're looking into it. This is clearly a message to Emily's family, and it's not a friendly one."

I knew I couldn't waste any time. I needed to follow up on Alicia's lead and find out more about Trevor. I asked Peter to keep me informed of any developments and left the scene, my determination renewed.

I drove to the bar outside town where Trevor worked. It was a dimly lit, rundown place with a few patrons scattered around, nursing their drinks. I spotted Trevor behind the counter, a tall man with dark hair and a scruffy beard. He looked to be in his early thirties, his eyes wary as they met mine.

I approached him, trying to appear casual. "Hello, Trevor. I'm Harper Bono, a retired detective. I'm looking into the disappearance of a young girl named Emily Johnson. I heard you might know something about it."

Trevor's eyes narrowed as he wiped down the counter. "I don't know what you're talking about," he said gruffly.

I could sense that Trevor was hiding something, but I needed to tread carefully. "Well, maybe you could tell me about The Lost Children," I suggested, watching his reaction closely.

His face paled, and his hands trembled slightly. "I don't know anything about that," he stammered. "Now, if you don't mind, I have work to do."

Before I could press further, my phone rang again. It was Peter. "Mr. Bono, we've found a connection between the vandalism and The Lost Children," he said. "We need you back at Emily's house immediately."

I quickly thanked Trevor for his time, making a mental note to return later. I drove back to Emily's house, my mind racing with questions. What was Trevor's connection to The Lost Children? What did the vandalism have to do with Emily's disappearance?

As I pulled up to the house, I saw that the police had cordoned off the area, and Peter was waiting for me outside.

Something bad happened again.

Chapter 5: The Secret and the Warning

Inside Emily's house, her parents stood by the open closet, their faces pale and shocked. I could see the fear in their eyes as they gestured toward a secret compartment that had been hidden behind Emily's clothes. Inside the compartment was an unusual altar, adorned with strange symbols and a different alphabet I couldn't recognize.

"What is this?" Robert asked, his voice trembling. "Why would Emily have this?"

I examined the altar closely, trying to decipher the symbols and the meaning behind them. As I studied the strange artifacts, my eyes were drawn to a small picture placed at the center of the altar. It was a picture of Trevor, the man I had spoken to earlier at the bar.

Before I could process this new discovery, a policewoman named Sally entered the room. She was an expert in unusual religious practices and had been called in to help with the investigation.

"This looks like a love spell," Sally said, examining the altar with keen interest. "It's meant to attract a specific person, in this case, Trevor. But I have to warn you, this type of magic can be dangerous if not performed correctly."

The revelation that Emily had been involved in such practices sent a shiver down my spine. I knew that we needed to focus on The Lost Children and their connection to Trevor, but this new information complicated the investigation even further.

I reassured Emily's parents that we would get to the bottom of this and find their daughter. I then left their house and set out to find Alicia, hoping she might have more information about Trevor and his possible connection to Emily's disappearance.

As I walked through the town, my phone buzzed with an incoming text message. It was from Monica. She asked me to return to my house and told me that she would stop by tonight to talk. However, she insisted that nobody should know about our meeting.

I agreed to her request, puzzled by the secrecy but eager to learn what she had to say. I couldn't help but wonder if Monica had information about Emily's secret altar or her connection to Trevor.

As evening fell, I returned to my house and prepared for Monica's arrival. I made some coffee and set out a plate of cookies, unsure of what to expect. The town was quiet, the darkness of the night pressing in around me, amplifying my sense of unease.

Finally, there was a knock at my door. I opened it to find Monica standing on my doorstep, her blond hair pulled back into a tight bun, her face pale and tense.

"Thank you for agreeing to meet with me, Mr. Bono," she said, her voice shaky. "I have something important to tell you about Emily and The Lost Children."

I ushered her inside, my curiosity piqued. As we sat down to talk, I couldn't help but feel that we were on the brink of uncovering a dark and dangerous secret, one that could finally lead us to Emily and the truth behind her disappearance.

But for now, all I could do was listen to Monica's story and hope that it would bring us one step closer to solving the mystery that had engulfed our small town. And as the night grew darker and the secrets began to unfold, I knew that, for some reason, nothing would ever be the same again.

Chapter 6: The Cult

Monica took a deep breath before she began her story, her hands tightly gripping the cup of coffee I had prepared for her. "The Lost Children," she said, "are a secret society that meets in a hut deep in the Blackroot Forest. Many people from our town are members, but they keep their involvement a secret. Some are ordinary people, like shopkeepers and teachers, while others hold positions of power. They all have one thing in common – they hide their true intentions behind friendly smiles."

I listened intently as Monica explained how she and Emily had started visiting the bar some years ago when they were just 14 years old. It was a daring adventure for the two young girls, a way to break free from the monotony of their small-town lives. That was where they met Trevor, a bartender with a warm smile and kind eyes. Emily quickly fell in love with him, but he didn't reciprocate her feelings. He was always kind and friendly, treating them nice as he always used to do.

"Emily became obsessed with Trevor," Monica continued, her voice cracking with emotion. "She couldn't accept that he didn't love her back. She thought that if she could just make him see how much she cared for him, he would change his mind. So she searched the internet for help and found someone who claimed he could make Trevor fall in love with her. His name was Luther."

Monica admitted that she had never met Luther, but she noticed a significant change in Emily after their interaction. Emily became secretive and distant, withdrawing from her friends and family. She began to spend more and more time alone in the forest, often returning late at night with dirt-streaked clothes and a haunted look in her eyes.

"Three days before she went missing, Emily and I had a huge fight," Monica confessed, tears welling up in her eyes. "I was worried about her and the path she was heading down, but she wouldn't listen to me. She accused me of being jealous and trying to sabotage her relationship with Trevor. I just wanted to help her, but she pushed me away."

I asked Monica if she had any more information about The Lost Children, Luther, or why she was afraid. She glanced around nervously, her gaze darting from window to window, as if expecting someone to be watching her.

"I feel like I'm being watched all the time," she whispered. "I think Emily saw something she shouldn't have in the forest, something related to The Lost Children. I don't know exactly what it was, but she seemed different after that – even more secretive and afraid. And now they're watching me too."

As Monica spoke, I couldn't help but think back to my conversation with Alicia, the old librarian who had first introduced me to the idea of The Lost Children. She had also warned me about the group's dangerous nature and the town's dark history of unsolved murders and disappearances. It was becoming increasingly clear that this secret society was involved in Emily's disappearance and that they might be keeping an eye on those who were getting too close to the truth.

Monica's revelation sent a chill down my spine, but I knew I couldn't let fear stop me from pursuing the truth. As our conversation came to an end, Monica looked at me with fear in her eyes. "You can't trust anyone, Mr. Bono. Not even the people you think you know. The Lost Children have eyes everywhere."

Just as she finished speaking, we heard a knock on the door. We exchanged nervous glances, both of us clearly on edge after our conversation. I got up from my chair and slowly approached the door, my heart pounding in my chest...

Chapter 7: Unraveling the Mystery

I opened the door, expecting to find someone lurking on my doorstep, but there was nobody there. The street outside was empty and eerily quiet. I closed the door, my heart still pounding from the adrenaline.

Monica decided it was time for her to leave. I thanked her for sharing her story and urged her to be careful. As she disappeared into the night, I couldn't help but feel that we were both in danger.

Alone in my house, I turned on my computer and began searching for similar cases of disappearances in the region. I found a few scattered reports, but they were miles away and didn't seem to be connected to Emily's case. I was about to give up when I stumbled across a church group with a similar name to "The Lost Children." Intrigued, I read further and discovered that they were a small community living in a nearby town, called the "The Lost Lambs".

The next day, I decided to pay them a visit. The church group's compound was nestled in a picturesque valley, surrounded by lush green hills. The people there lived a simple, communal lifestyle, reminiscent of the hippie movement from decades past. They grew their own food, wore handmade clothes, and seemed to live in harmony with nature.

I was greeted by their leader, Dr. Samuel, a charismatic and well-spoken man in his sixties. He welcomed me into his home and offered me a cup of herbal tea. As we sipped our drinks, I asked him about the history of their community and its connection to the name "The Lost Children."

Dr. Samuel explained that 50 years ago, there were certain individuals who sought to change the character of their community. They engaged in troubling behavior, including animal sacrifices and other dark rituals. The community had no choice but to banish them, and since then, they hadn't heard anything about their whereabouts or activities.

As I listened to Dr. Samuel's story, I couldn't help but wonder if these outcasts were the same people who had formed the weird cult in our town. The timing and the name were too much of a coincidence to ignore.

I showed Dr. Samuel a picture of Emily, and his face lit up with recognition. He told me that she had visited their community a few months back, accompanied by an older man. She had been asking questions about their way of life, but her demeanor was strange – ironic and mean-spirited, as if she was mocking them. Dr. Samuel didn't know who the older man was, but he did mention that Emily seemed to be under his influence.

Armed with this new information, I returned to our town and shared my findings with Peter. We both agreed that there must be a connection between Emily's disappearance and the outcasts from Dr. Samuel's community.

As we discussed our next steps, my phone rang. It was Alicia, her voice urgent and breathless. "Bono, you need to come to my house right away," she said. "I've found something important."

I didn't waste any time. I jumped into my car and sped toward Alicia's house, my mind racing with possibilities. Was this the breakthrough we needed to find Emily? Or was it another piece of the puzzle, leading us further into the darkness?

As I pulled up outside Alicia's house, I noticed that the door was slightly ajar. I hesitated for a moment, recalling Monica's warning not to trust anyone. But I couldn't ignore Alicia's plea for help, so I steeled myself and entered her home, ready to face whatever awaited me inside.

Chapter 8: A House of Horrors

As I stepped inside Alicia's house, I was struck by the chaos that greeted me. It was as if nature had invaded her home, reclaiming it as its own. Branches, dust, and flowers covered every surface, and mushrooms sprouted from the walls, their caps stretching upwards as they sought light in the dimly lit room. It was both beautiful and terrifying, an eerie, surreal landscape that seemed to defy reality.

I carefully picked my way through the debris, trying to make sense of what had happened here. The destruction was so complete, so thorough, that it seemed like the work of a force far greater than any human could wield. But there was no time to ponder the cause – I needed to find Alicia.

As I searched the house, I couldn't shake the feeling that I was being watched. The air was thick with tension, the silence punctuated only by the creaking of the floorboards beneath my feet and the distant rustling of leaves outside. I felt a growing sense of dread with each passing moment, knowing that I was venturing deeper into danger.

Finally, I reached the last room of the house and as I pushedthe door open, my heart caught in my throat. There, hanging from a bush, was a portrait of a girl with red hair – Emily. The portrait was tightly bound with rope, and a trail of gasoline led from its base to a pile of kindling in the corner. It was clear that someone had been preparing to set the portrait on fire.

I stood there, frozen in horror, as the implications of the scene sank in. Was this a message? A warning? And where was Alicia? I pulled out my phone and dialed the police, my hands shaking as I relayed the details of what I had found.

As I hung up, I caught a glimpse of movement out of the corner of my eye. A shadowy figure darted through the house, clearly trying to escape. Adrenaline surged through my veins, and I took off after them, determined to catch the person responsible for the destruction and terror I had witnessed.

The manhunt was intense, a game of cat and mouse through the wrecked house and into the surrounding woods. Every time I thought I had the figure cornered, they managed to slip away, their movements quick and agile.

Finally, I managed to lead the figure to a dead-end, a small clearing surrounded by dense underbrush. I lunged at them, my body colliding with theirs as we both tumbled to the ground. We fought fiercely, our limbs tangled in a desperate struggle for control.

With a final burst of strength, I managed to pin the figure down and pulled their full-face mask off, revealing the face underneath. To my shock and disbelief, it was the policewoman from Emily's house – Sally.

My mind raced as I tried to make sense of this revelation. What was her connection to The Lost Children? Was she involved in Emily's disappearance? And where was Alicia?

As these questions swirled in my mind, I heard the distant sound of sirens approaching. The police had arrived. I held Sally in place, my grip firm and unyielding, as I waited for them to take her into custody. I knew that this was just the beginning of a much larger mystery, and I was more determined than ever to uncover the truth.

Chapter 9: The Interrogation

The interrogation room was cold and sterile, its white walls and harsh lighting creating an atmosphere of unease. I stood behind the one-way mirror, watching as Peter and a younger colleague, Max, faced Sally, the policewoman we had apprehended in Alicia's home. The tension in the room was palpable, a heavy weight that hung over us all.

For the first few minutes, Sally said nothing. She stared straight ahead, her expression blank and unreadable. Peter and Max fired question after question at her, but she remained silent, unresponsive to their increasingly desperate attempts to get her to talk.

Finally, after what felt like an eternity, Sally spoke. "Alicia is dead," she said, her voice cold and emotionless. "I don't know where they took her."

The room seemed to grow even colder at her words. Peter and Max exchanged uneasy glances before continuing their questioning. They asked her about the bizarre scene we had discovered at Alicia's house, the explosion of nature that seemed to defy all logic.

Sally's eyes seemed to darken as she described the abilities of The Lost Children. "They can do magic," she said, her voice low and haunting. "They can make things grow, even when they shouldn't be able to. It's their power, their gift."

Everyone in the room was taken aback by her words, unsure of how to process the idea of magic and supernatural abilities. The thought that such a cult could exist, and that they might be responsible for Emily's disappearance, was both terrifying and bewildering.

Sally's gaze suddenly shifted, and she stared directly at the one-way mirror, her eyes locked onto mine as if she could see through the glass. "Bono has caused The Lost Children much trouble," she said, her voice taking on an eerie, otherworldly quality. "They are looking for him."

Enraged and frightened by her words, I burst into the interrogation room, my hands balled into fists. "I'm not afraid of you or The Lost Children!" I shouted, my voice shaking with anger and fear. "You'll pay for what you've done!"

Sally just laughed, a chilling sound that echoed through the room. Her laughter grew louder and more maniacal, and then, without warning, she slumped forward in her chair, unconscious.

At that moment, the walls of the police station began to creak and groan, and branches started to burst through the plaster, their tendrils snaking through the air as they grew at an unnatural speed. Panic erupted as officers scrambled to escape the room, their guns drawn as they fired wildly at the advancing branches.

The chaos was overwhelming, a cacophony of gunfire, shouting, and the relentless advance of nature as it tore through the walls of the once-safe haven of the police station. I stood in the midst of it all, my heart pounding in my chest, knowing that I had been drawn into a conflict far greater and more terrifying than I could have ever imagined.

As the branches continued to grow, it became clear that we were up against an enemy that defied all reason and understanding. The Lost Children were more than just a secret society or a cult – they were a force to be reckoned with, and they would stop at nothing to achieve their goals.

Determined to put an end to their reign of terror, I knew that I had no choice but to face them head-on, to delve deeper into the darkness and uncover the truth about their mysterious powers and their connection to Emily's disappearance. And as I stared down the barrel of the unknown, I couldn't help but wonder if I would be able to emerge unscathed, or if I, too, would become one of the Lost Children's many victims.

Chapter 10: Into the Forest

As I stepped out of the police station, the devastation caused by the branches was apparent. They had grown throughout the entire city, spreading panic and chaos among the citizens who now filled the streets. Cars were abandoned, their windows shattered by the relentless advance of nature, and people were running in fear, desperate to escape the surreal scene that had unfolded before them.

It was then that I saw Monica and Trevor approaching me, their faces a mix of determination and concern. They had evidently seen the destruction firsthand and knew that they needed to help.

"Did you see what's happening?" Monica asked, her voice shaking slightly. "We need to do something, Bono."

Trevor nodded, adding, "We can't just stand here and watch our town fall apart."

Together, we climbed into my car, our minds focused on the task at hand. As we drove through the chaotic streets, we began to discuss the situation.

Trevor spoke up, "I've seen The Lost Children's camp in the forest while hunting with my father. We could start there."

Monica, her voice filled with conviction, insisted, "Emily is still alive, I know it. We need to find her and put an end to this."

I shared with them my experience at Alicia's house and the terrifying portrait I had discovered. "I found this portrait of a girl, just like Emily, bound and ready to be set on fire," I said, my voice somber.

Monica's expression hardened, and she clenched her fists. "That means Emily is in real danger. We have to hurry."

The three of us continued to drive, leaving the chaos of the city behind as we ventured deeper into the forest. The road eventually gave way to a dirt path, and we were forced to abandon the car and continue on foot.

"We need to be careful and stay quiet," Trevor warned as he led the way. "We don't want them to know we're coming."

As we trekked through the woods, the shadows grew longer, and the air colder. The forest seemed to close in around us, its branches reaching out like gnarled fingers, as if trying to ensnare us in their grasp. But we pressed on, guided by our shared determination to put an end to the madness that had gripped our city.

As we walked, we discussed our plan of action. "We should approach the camp cautiously," I suggested. "Gather as much information as possible, and then figure out a plan to rescue Emily and put a stop to the cult's activities."

Monica agreed, adding, "We need to save her, and anyone else who might be trapped there."

Hours passed as we made our way deeper into the forest, the light of day fading until all that remained was the pale glow of the moon filtering through the trees. We moved as quietly as possible, acutely aware of the need for stealth as we neared our destination.

Finally, after what felt like an eternity, we spotted the camp ahead. It was just as Trevor had described – a collection of tents and makeshift shelters, a sinister presence in the heart of the forest. We paused at the edge of the clearing, taking in the sight before us and steeling ourselves for what lay ahead.

"Alright," I whispered, "let's do this. But remember, stay quiet and stay together."

Together, we stepped out of the shadows and into the clearing, our hearts pounding in our chests as we moved closer to the unknown dangers that awaited us within The Lost Children's camp.

Chapter 11: The Confrontation

Upon entering the camp, we found it eerily quiet and seemingly abandoned. Everything looked relatively normal, save for a large pile of wood and torn bushes in the center of the camp. As our eyes adjusted to the dim light, we spotted a cage near the pile, and inside it was Emily, unconscious but appearing to sleep peacefully like an angel.

Monica and Trevor rushed towards her, but as they neared the cage, branches shot out from the pile of wood and bushes, ensnaring them like chains. They struggled in vain, but the more they fought, the tighter the branches became.

I stood frozen in place for a moment, then reached for my gun, only to realize there was nothing I could shoot that would help my friends. It was then that at least ten people dressed in black gowns and hoods emerged from the shadows behind the trees, chanting in a haunting chorus. In their midst was an old man with a long white beard, who appeared to be their leader.

"Who are you?" I demanded, my voice shaking with fear and anger.

The old man, his eyes fixed on me, replied, "I am the founder of The Lost Children. People call me Luther".

As we stared each other down, he revealed that he was the one who had promised Emily a love potion for Trevor. The old man explained that he possessed the power to make things grow, but in order for his abilities to evolve, he needed to perform human sacrifices.

"We have been moving from place to place for many years, living like nomads," he said. "We've traveled across the world, seeking the 'Lost Children' who would join our cause. And now, we have finally found a place where we can settle down and call home. But first, your city must be destroyed."

I glared at him, my heart pounding in my chest. "I can't let you do this," I growled.

With a mere snap of his fingers, the old man caused me to fall to the ground, immobilized. I felt my skin sprouting mushrooms and leaves, dirt filling my mouth, and roots creeping down my throat. Desperately trying to breathe, I could do nothing but watch as the townspeople I had come to know emerged from the shadows, their eyes dark and cold.

The old man walked towards me, stopping just inches from my face. "Do you understand now, Bono? You cannot stop us."

As I lay there, struggling to draw breath, I mustered the strength to whisper, "You're wrong. I won't let you win."

He laughed, a chilling sound that echoed through the forest. "You have no choice, detective. You are powerless."

But even as I lay there, trapped in the old man's spell, a glimmer of hope shone in the darkness. I remembered the words of Monica, who had urged me to trust no one. And in that moment, I realized that she was right: the only person I could truly rely on was myself.

Gathering every ounce of strength I had left, I focused my thoughts on breaking free from the old man's grasp. To my amazement, the roots in my throat began to recede, the mushrooms and leaves disappearing from my skin.

The old man's eyes widened in shock as he witnessed my transformation. "No," he whispered, "it's not possible."

But I knew that it was. And as I stood up, pushing past the pain and the fear, I faced Luther and the townrs, my resolve unwavering.

"I will not let you destroy our town," I declared. "And I will not let you harm any more innocent people."

Chapter 12: The Escape

I took aim and fired my gun at Luther, the bullet tearing through his chest. As he crumpled to the ground, Trevor fought off the branches that held him captive, breaking free and rushing towards Emily's cage.

Monica, meanwhile, grabbed a torch from one of the Lost Children and began to swing it wildly, striking any cult member who came too close. She fought ferociously, her determination clear in her eyes.

Trevor managed to reach Emily and, using the butt of his gun, shattered the lock on her cage. He gently lifted her limp body into his arms, cradling her protectively as we began to make our escape.

Monica, still wielding the torch, led the way through the forest. As we sprinted past the campsite, she hurled the flaming torch onto a pile of dry leaves. The fire quickly spread, engulfing two nearby tents in a blaze.

The encampment erupted in a tumultuous symphony of sound and fire as we fled, the intense blaze chasing us away from the scene. Trevor carried Emily, her head lolling against his shoulder as we made our way through the dense forest. Our hearts pounded in our chests, our breath ragged and desperate, but we didn't dare stop running.

In the distance, we spotted a group of torches, their light flickering through the darkness. As we drew nearer, we realized that it was a search party led by Peter, who had come looking for us.

Upon reaching the group, Peter caught me just as my legs gave out, exhaustion and pain threatening to overwhelm me. The last thing I remember before falling unconcious was the sound of Peter's voice, reassuring me that we were safe.

When I awoke, I found myself lying in a hospital bed, the sterile white walls and steady beeping of machines a stark contrast to the chaos of the forest. A pretty nurse stood at my bedside, her eyes filled with concern.

"Are you alright?" she asked, her voice gentle and soothing.

I nodded, my throat dry and raw. "What happened?" I croaked, struggling to sit up.

"You and your friends were found in the forest," she explained. "You were in pretty bad shape, but you're going to be okay. Everyone's been asking about you."

Relief washed over me as I realized that we had escaped the clutches of the Lost Children. Monica, Trevor, and Emily were safe, and the town was no longer under the threat of destruction.

As the nurse continued to check on me and update me on the condition of my friends, I couldn't help but feel a deep sense of gratitude

The town would recover, slowly healing from the wounds inflicted by the cult. And though the memories of our ordeal would never fade, we had emerged stronger and more united than ever before. At least that's how I felt.

The sun began to rise outside my hospital window, casting warm golden light across the room. It was a new day. I closed my eyes and allowed myself to drift back to sleep, knowing that when I awoke, I would be ready to face the world once more.

Chapter 13: Unsettling Revelations

After my recovery, I was eager to see Emily and learn how she was doing. I found her in the next room, surrounded by Monica and Trevor. As I entered, they greeted me with warm smiles and tight hugs.

Emily was a bit shy, but she looked at me with deep gratitude. "Thank you," she whispered, her voice barely audible. "I'm so sorry for everything that happened."

Tears filled her eyes as she recounted her story. She explained that the cult members had used their magic to control her mind, bending her to their will. At first, they had tried to convince her to join a peaceful community, but the elder there had refused. In response, the cult decided to destroy Willowbrook, believing that Emily's powers would help them achieve their goal.

As Emily sobbed, I tried to comfort her. "You were brave, and the nightmare is over now," I assured her. Her family and friends were safe, and the Lost Children's influence had been severed.

A few days later, I was discharged from the hospital and returned to my house. The memories of my time in the town now weighed heavily on my mind, and I decided that it was time for me to leave.

Peter called to thank me for my help and pleaded with me to stay, insisting that I was an asset to the police force. I was touched by his words but knew that I couldn't remain in a place that held so many dark memories.

As I packed my belongings, I glanced out the window and noticed a figure standing by the edge of the fence, right at the entrance of the forest. My heart skipped a beat as I recognized Alicia, her face pale and her expression wild. She stared at me, an eerie smile playing across her lips.

I watched in horror as she blinked and vanished, leaving only a growing tree in her place. My mind raced as I realized the truth: Alicia hadn't died but had been orchestrating the events from the very beginning. The realization sent chills down my spine, and I knew that I had to do something.

I called Peter immediately, my voice shaking as I shared my discovery. He promised to launch an investigation, but I knew that the task wouldn't be easy. Alicia had used her magic to deceive and manipulate us all, and there was no telling what she would do next.

I decided to stay in the town for a little while longer, determined to see the case through to its conclusion. I couldn't allow Alicia to remain a threat to the people I had come to care about.

As the days turned into weeks, we searched tirelessly for any trace of Alicia. We interviewed a bunch of people, dug through archives, and scoured the forest, but she remained elusive. It seemed as if she had vanished into thin air, leaving only fear and uncertainty in her wake.

Despite the challenges, I couldn't shake the feeling that we were on the right path. Alicia's actions had been horrifying, but they had also brought the community closer together. People were more vigilant, more supportive of one another, and more determined than ever to protect their home.

I can’t say for certain what the future holds, but I know that the town will never be the same again. The darkness that had once lurked beneath the surface is now exposed, and we all have to face it together.

As I’m standing at my window, looking out at the tree that has grown in Alicia's place, I feel a strange mixture of fear and excitement. I know that I’ll never truly be free of the shadow of the Lost Children, but I also know that I will never stop fighting to keep the people I care about safe.

And so, with renewed purpose, I turn away from the window, make some black coffee and get myself ready to face a new day in Willowbrook.

THE END

PRACTICE

Exercise 1: Match the words with their definitions

Vandalism
Disappearances
Cult
Secret society
Red-haired
Interrogation
Possessed
Nomads
Hippies
Manhunt
Definitions:

a. A group of people who live a simple, non-materialistic lifestyle, often embracing peace and love
b. People who have no permanent home and move from place to place in search of food, water, and grazing land
c. The act of intentionally causing damage to public or private property, often for no apparent reason
d. The action or an instance of forcefully questioning someone, especially a suspect or a prisoner
e. A group of people with a common belief, typically religious, and often living in an isolated community under the guidance of a charismatic leader
f. An organized search for a criminal, typically by police
g. Influenced or controlled by an evil spirit or supernatural force
h. Having red-colored hair
i. A group of people who share a secret or exclusive knowledge and purpose, often with the intent of gaining power or influence
j. Instances of people going missing, often without explanation or trace

Exercise 2: Choose the appropriate vocabulary word from exercise 1 to complete the sentences.

The police launched a massive _______ after the dangerous criminal escaped from prison.
The ancient _______ worshipped a deity that no one had ever heard of before.
The painting was ruined due to an act of _______ by an unknown individual.
The _______ room was dimly lit, and the suspect began to feel anxious as the questioning began.
Some people believe that the world is secretly controlled by a _______ that manipulates global events.
The family was known for their striking _______ hair, which set them apart from the rest of the townrs.
The tribe of _______ traveled through the desert, following the path of the seasonal rains.
The sudden _______ of several people from the small town raised concerns among the residents.
The young woman seemed to be _______ by a malevolent spirit, causing her to act strangely and violently.
The group of _______ lived in a commune, sharing their resources and promoting peace and harmony.

Exercise 3: Write a sentence using each of the vocabulary words below:

Vandalism:
Disappearances:
Cult:
Secret society:
Red-haired:
Interrogation:
Possessed:
Nomads:
Hippies:

Manhunt:

Exercise 4: Answer the following questions:

What did Harper Bono find at the end of Chapter 1 that led him to investigate Emily's disappearance?

Who is Alicia, and what information does she share about the history of the town and the "Lost Children"?

Describe the atmosphere in Emily's house when Bono visits her family.

Why is Monica scared and why does she feel like she's being watched?

What did Bono discover about the group with a similar name to the "Lost Children"?

How did Bono manage to capture the policewoman responsible for the vandalism at Emily's house?

What was the woman's connection to the "Lost Children" and what did she reveal about their powers?

How did Monica, Trevor, and Bono escape from the "Lost Children" camp in the forest?

What did Emily reveal about her involvement with the "Lost Children" and their plan for the town?

In the final chapter, what shocking realization did Bono have about Alicia's true identity and involvement in the events?

Exercise 5: Complete the writing tasks below:

A. Imagine you are Harper Bono. Write a journal entry describing your feelings and thoughts when you first moved to the town and discovered the flyer of the missing girl.

B. Write a letter from Monica to Emily, expressing her concern about Emily's behavior after meeting Luther and her involvement with the "Lost Children."

C. Write a conversation between Bono and Peter, discussing their suspicions about the mysterious events happening in the town and their plan to investigate further.

D. Pretend you are a member of the "Lost Children" cult. Write a diary entry describing a typical day in the cult and your thoughts about its activities and beliefs.

E. Write a newspaper article about the strange events in the town, including the disappearance of Emily, the vandalism at her house, and the mysterious "Lost Children" cult.

F. Imagine you are Emily after being rescued. Write a letter to Bono, thanking him for saving her and expressing her regret for her actions under the influence of the "Lost Children."

G. Write a dialogue between Bono and Alicia, confronting her about her true identity and her involvement in the events that transpired in the town.

H. Create a monologue from Bono's perspective, reflecting on his experiences in the town, the people he met, and what he learned from the events that unfolded.

I. Write a short story about another mysterious case that Harper Bono investigates, using the themes and characters from the original story.

J. Write an alternative ending for the story, where the "Lost Children" cult is exposed, and the town comes together to rebuild and heal from the events that took place.

CPSIA information can be obtained
at www.ICGtesting.com
Printed in the USA
LVHW052008150623
749895LV00003B/288